Adventures in Storytelling

MW01178545

The Baboon's Umbrella

An African Folktale

Illustrated by

Ching

CHILDRENS PRESS ®
CHICAGO

Adventures in Storytelling

Dear Parents and Teachers,

Adventures in Storytelling Books have been designed to delight storytellers of all ages and to make world literature available to non-readers as well as to those who speak English as a second language. The wordless format and accompanying audiocassette make it possible for both readers and nonreaders who are unacquainted with a specific ethnic folktale to use either the visual or the audio portion as an aid in understanding the story.

For additional reference the complete story text is printed in the back of the book, and post-story activities are suggested for those who enjoy more participation.

The history of storytelling

"Once upon a time...."

"Long ago but not so long ago that we cannot remember...."

"In the grey, grey beginnings of the world...."

"And it came to pass, more years ago than I can tell you...."

These are magic words. They open kingdoms and countries beyond our personal experiences and make the impossible possible and the miraculous, if not commonplace, at least not unexpected.

For hundreds of years people have been telling stories. You do it every day, every time you say, "You'll never believe what happened to me yesterday"; or "You know, something like that happened to my grandmother, but according to her, it went something like this...."

Before video recorders, tape recorders, television, and radio, there was storytelling. It was the vehicle through which every culture remembered its past and kept alive its heritage. It was the way people explained life, shared events, and entertained themselves around the fire on dark, lonely nights. The stories they told evoked awe and respect for tradition, ritual, wisdom, and power; transmitted cultural taboos and teachings from generation to generation; and made people laugh at the foolishness in life or cry when confronted by life's tragedies.

As every culture had its stories, so too did each have its story-tellers. In Africa they were called griots; in Ireland, seanachies; in France, troubadours; and in the majority of small towns and villages around the world they were simply known as the gifted. Often their stories were hundreds of years old. Some of them were told exactly as they had been told for centuries; others were changed often to reflect people's interests and where and how they lived.

With the coming of the printing press and the availability of printed texts, the traditional storyteller began to disappear — not altogether and not everywhere, however. There were pockets in the world where stories were kept alive by those who remembered them and believed in them. Although not traditional storytellers, these people continued to pass down folktales, even though the need for formal, professional storytelling was fading.

In the nineteenth century, the Grimm brothers made the folk-tale fashionable, and for the first time collections of tales from many countries became popular. Story collections by Andrew Lang, Joseph Jacobs, and Charles Perrault became the rage, with one important difference: these stories were written down to be read, not told aloud to be heard.

As the nineteenth century gave way to the twentieth, there was a revival of interest in storytelling. Spearheaded by children's librarians and schoolteachers, a new kind of storytelling evolved — one that was aimed specifically at children and connected to literature and reading. The form of literature most chosen by these librarians and teachers was the traditional folktale.

During this time prominent educator May Hill Arbuthnot wrote that children were a natural audience for folktales because the qualities found in these tales were those to which children normally responded in stories: brisk action, humor, and an appeal to a sense of justice. Later, folklorist Max Luthi supported this theory. He called the folktale a fundamental building block, an outstanding aid in child development, and the archetypal form of literature that lays the groundwork for all literature.

By the middle of the twentieth century, storytelling was seen as a way of exposing children to literature that they would not discover by themselves and of making written language accessible to those who could not read it by themselves. Storytelling became a method of promoting an understanding of other cultures and a means of strengthening the cultural awareness of the listening group; a way of creating that community of listeners that evolves when a diverse group listens to a tale well-told.

Many of these same reasons for storytelling are valid today — perhaps even more relevant than they were nearly one hundred years ago. Current research confirms what librarians and teachers have known all along — that storytelling provides a practical, effective, and enjoyable way to introduce children to literature while fostering a love of reading. It connects the child to the story and the book. Through storytelling, great literature (the classics, poetry, traditional folktales) comes alive; children learn to love language and experience the beauty of the spoken word, often before they master those words by reading them themselves.

Without exception, all cultures have accumulated a body of folktales that represent their history, beliefs, and language. Yet, while each culture's folktales are unique, they also are connected to the folktales of other cultures through the universality of themes contained within them. Some of the most common themes appearing in folktales around the world deal with good overcoming evil; the clever outwitting the strong; and happiness being the reward for kindness to strangers, the elderly, and the less fortunate. We hear these themes repeated in stories from quaint Irish villages along the Atlantic coast to tiny communities spread throughout the African veldt and from cities and towns of the industrialized Americas to the magnificent palaces of the emperors of China and Japan. It is these similarities that are fascinating; that help us to transcend the barriers of language, politics, custom, and religion; and that bind us together as "the folk" in folktales.

Using wordless picture books and audiocassettes

Every child is a natural storyteller. Children begin telling stories almost as soon as they learn to speak. The need to share what they experience and how they perceive life prompts them to organize their thoughts and express themselves in a way others will understand. But storytelling goes beyond the everyday need to communicate. Beyond the useful, storytelling can be developed into a skill that entertains and teaches. Using wordless picture books and audiocassettes aids in this process.

When children hear a story told, they are learning much about language, story structure, plot development, words, and the development of a "sense of story." Wordless books encourage readers to focus on pictures for the story line and the sequence of events, which builds children's visual skills. In time, the "visually literate" child will find it easier to develop verbal and written skills.

Because a wordless folktale book is not restricted by reading ability or educational level, it can be used as a tool in helping children and adults, both English and non-English speakers, as well as readers and nonreaders to understand or retell a story from their own rich, ethnic perspective. Listening to folktales told on an audiocassette or in person offers another advantage; it allows the listener, who may be restricted by reading limitations, to enjoy literature, learn about other cultures, and develop essential prereading skills. Furthermore, it gives them confidence to retell stories on their own and motivates them to learn to read them.

Something special happens when you tell a story; something special happens when you hear a story well-told. Storytelling is a unique, entertaining, and powerful art form, one that creates an intimate bond between storyteller and listener, past and present. To take a story and give it a new voice is an exhilarating experience; to watch someone else take that same story and make it his or her own is another.

Janice M. Del Negro
Children's Services
The Chicago Public Library

The following tale is a familiar African fable about a baboon who, in an effort to protect himself from the rain, follows the foolish advice of a friend. In the end, he finds that he has not solved his problem at all.

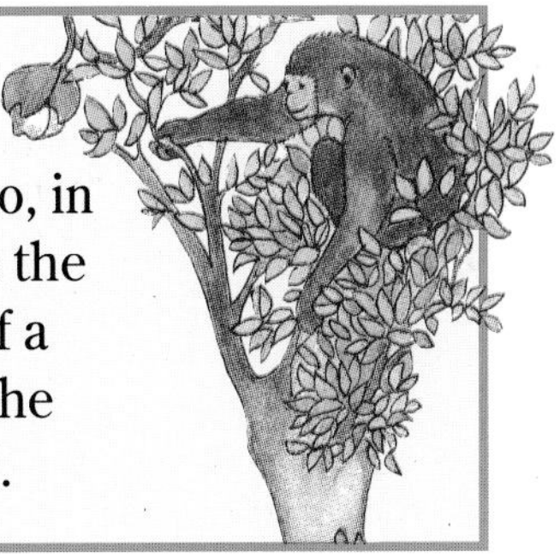

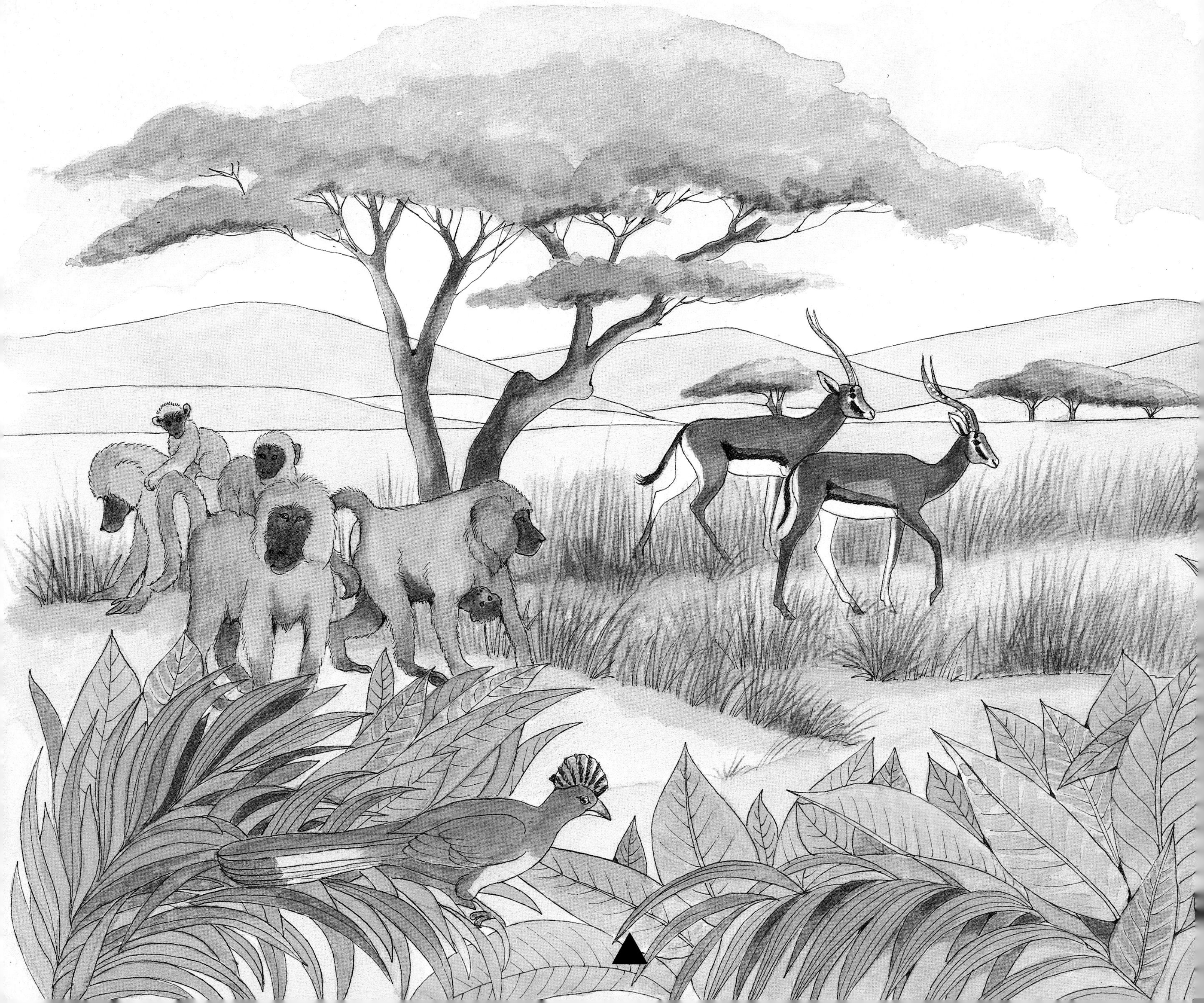

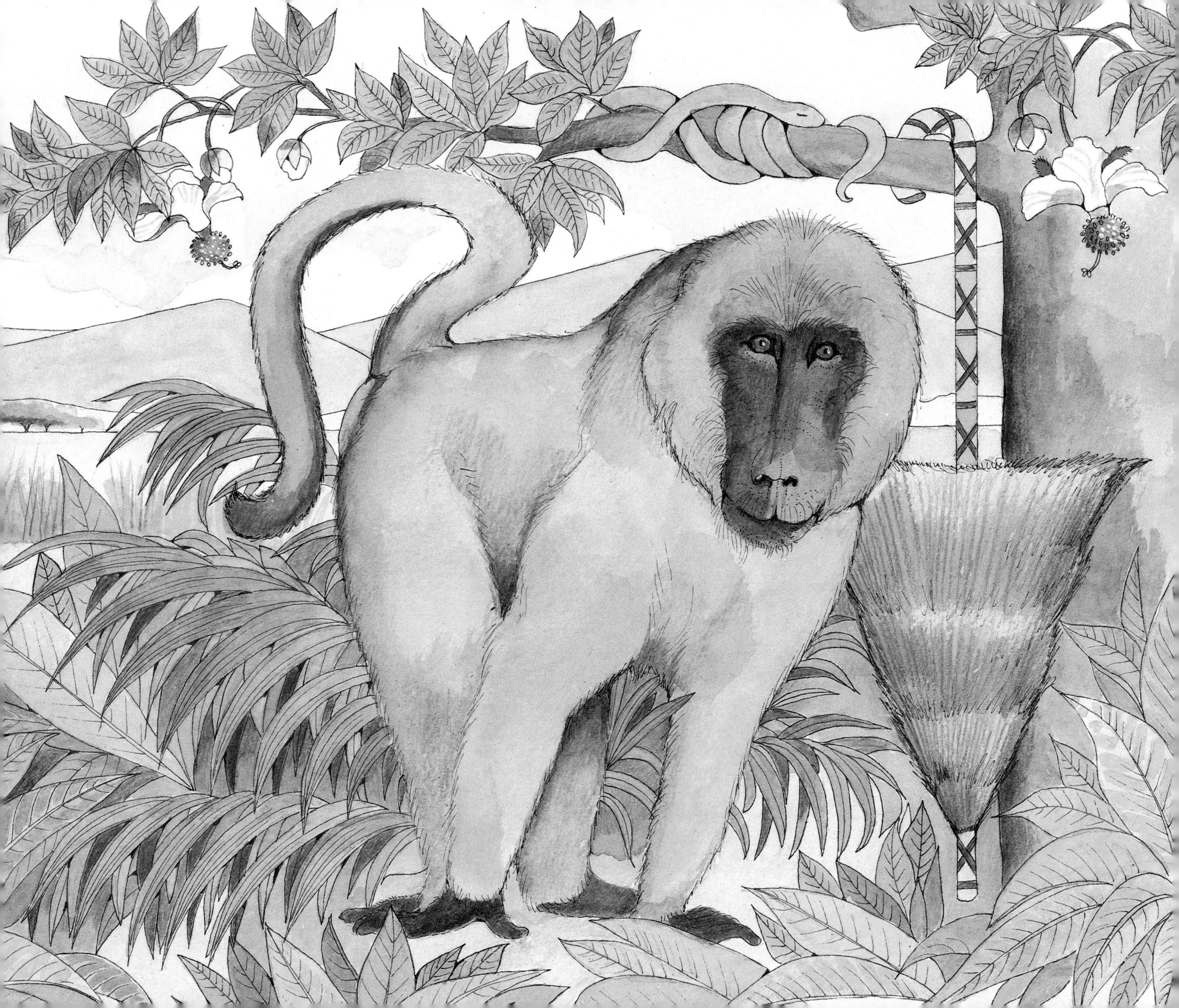

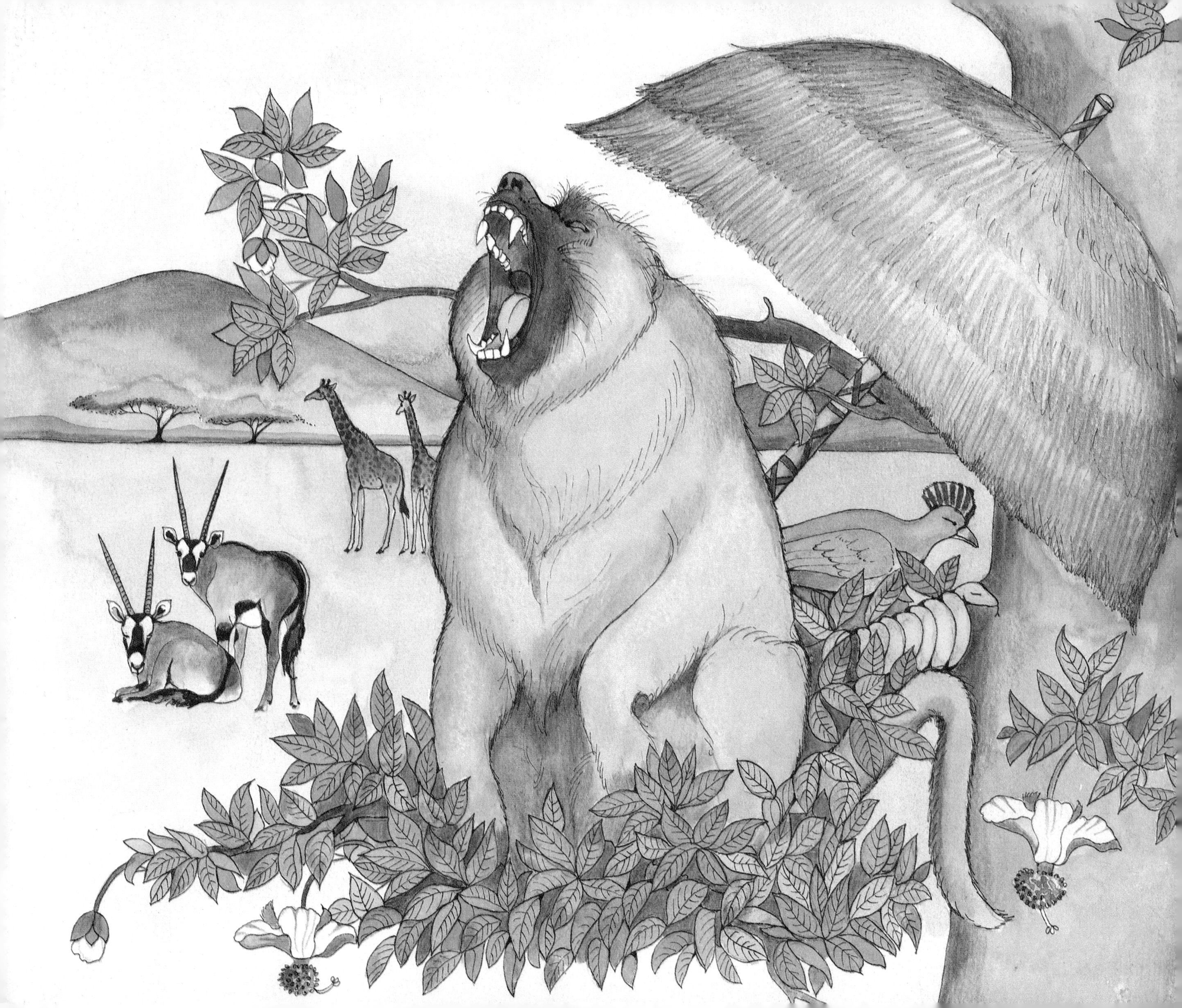

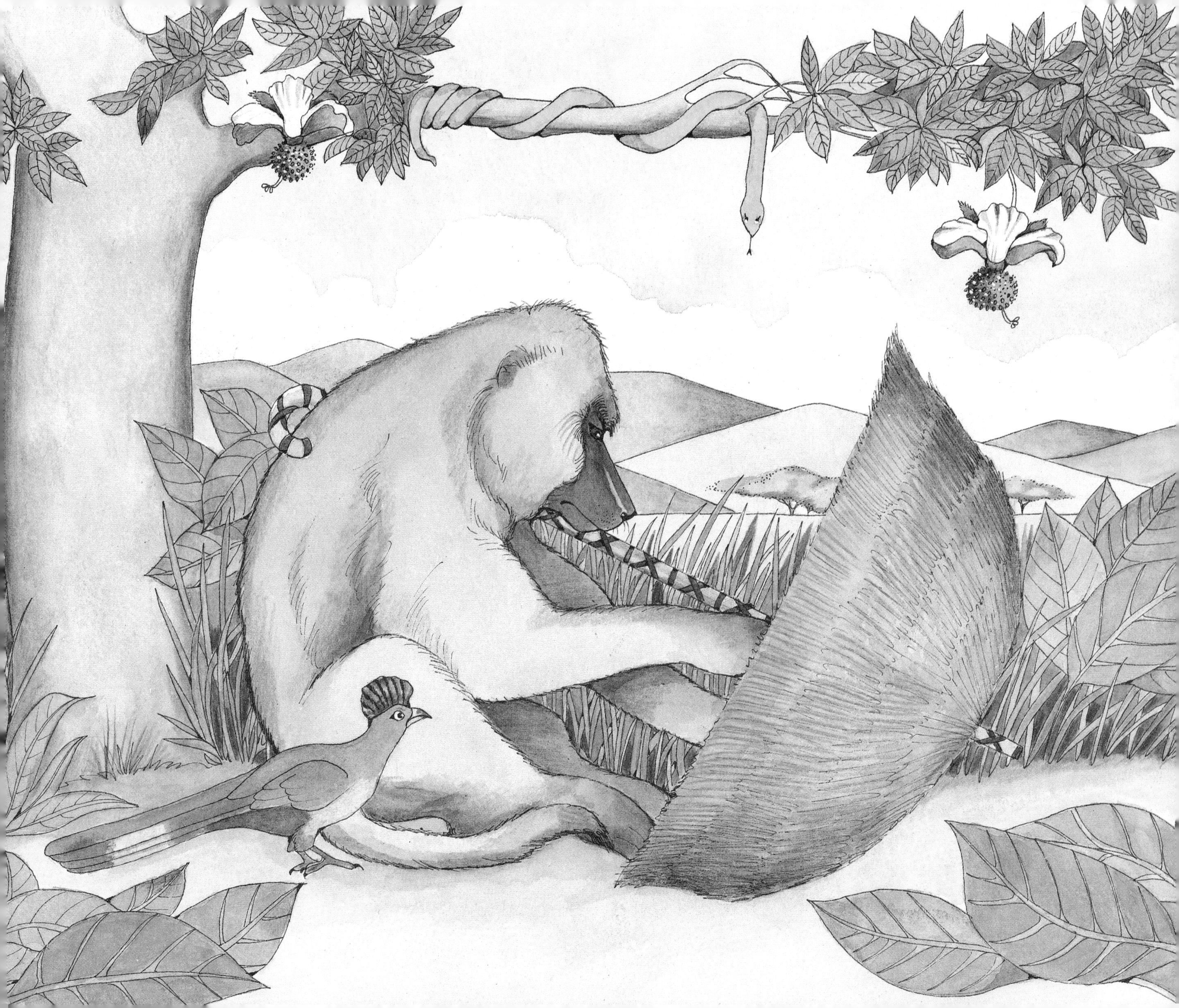

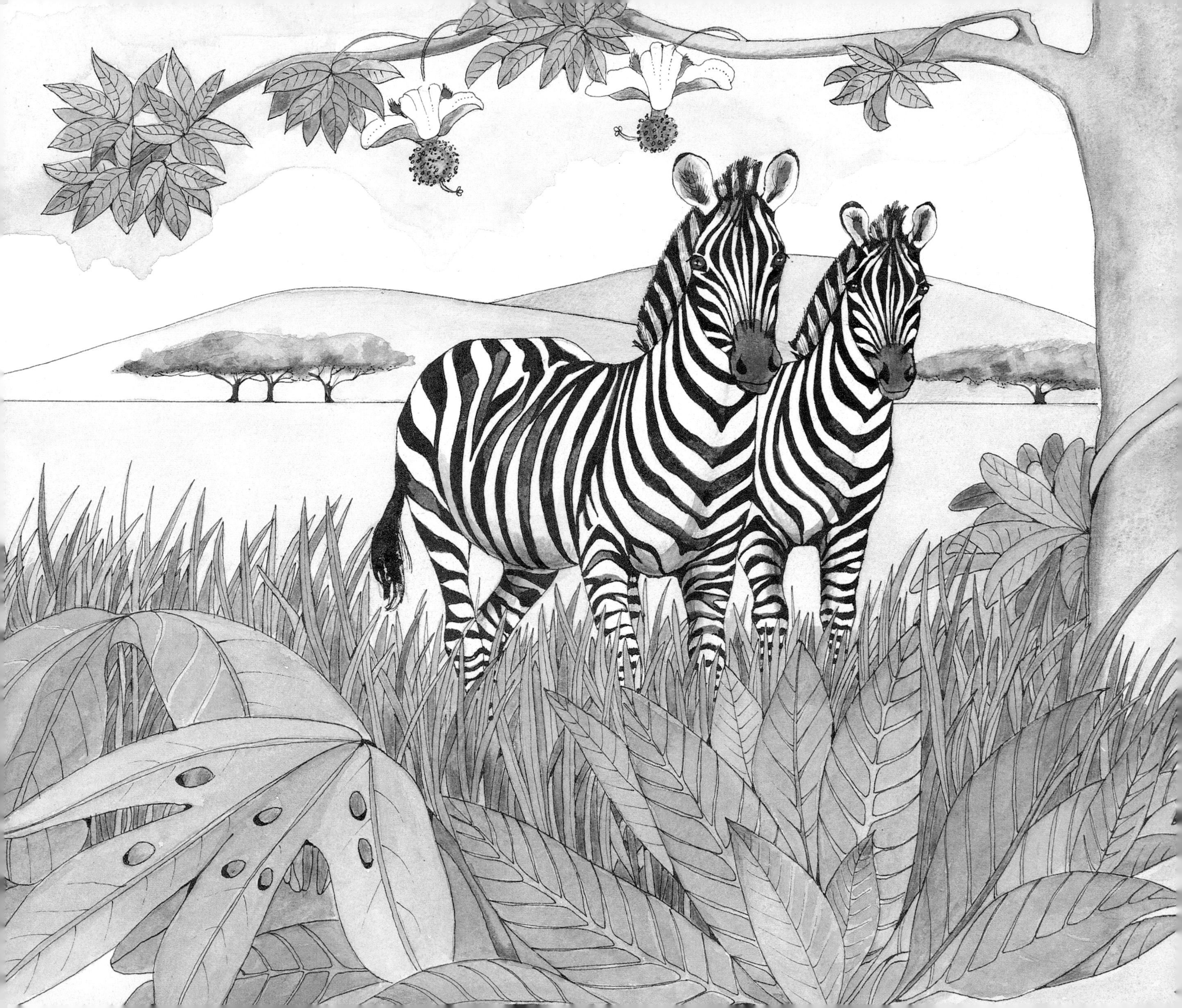

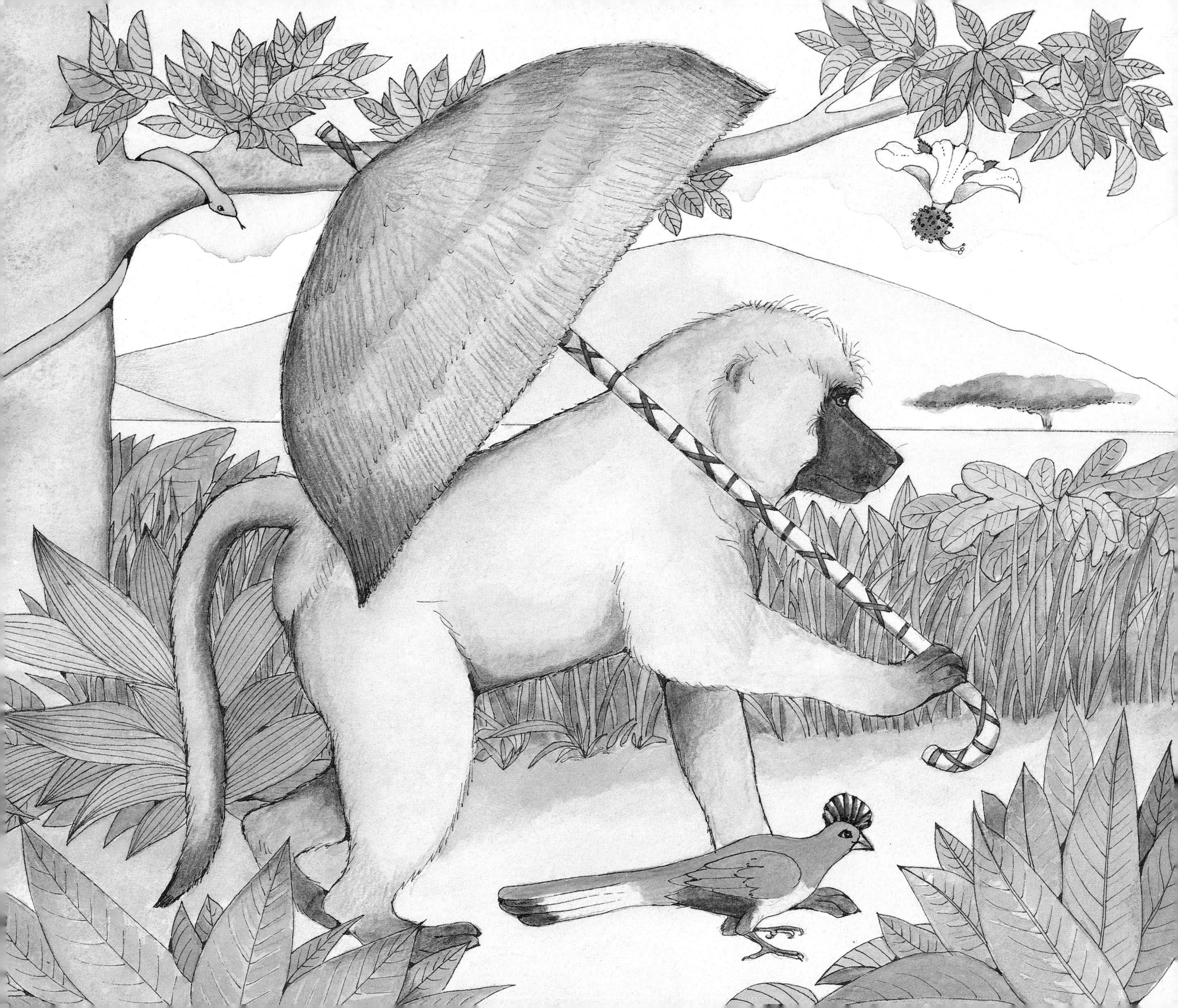

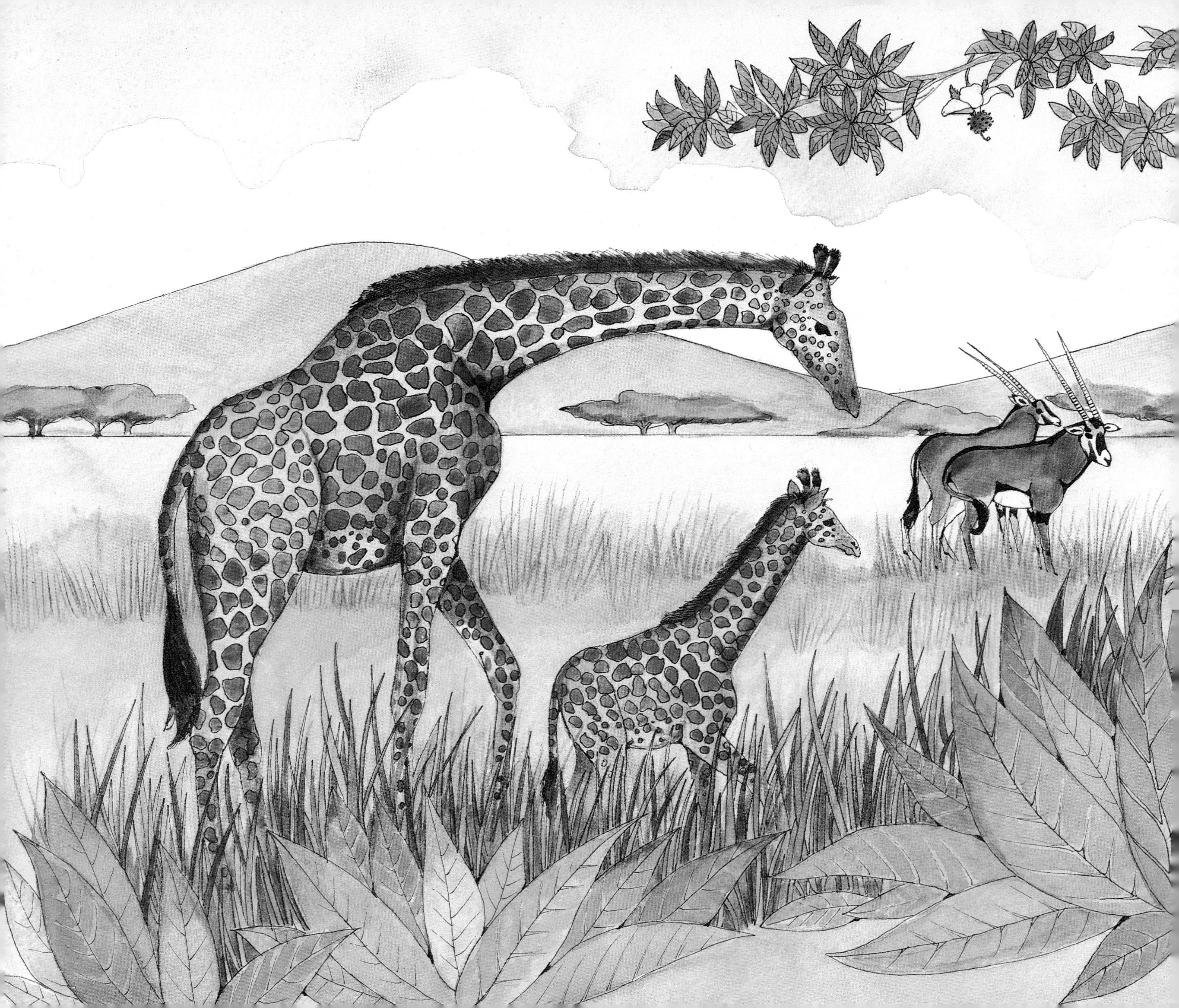

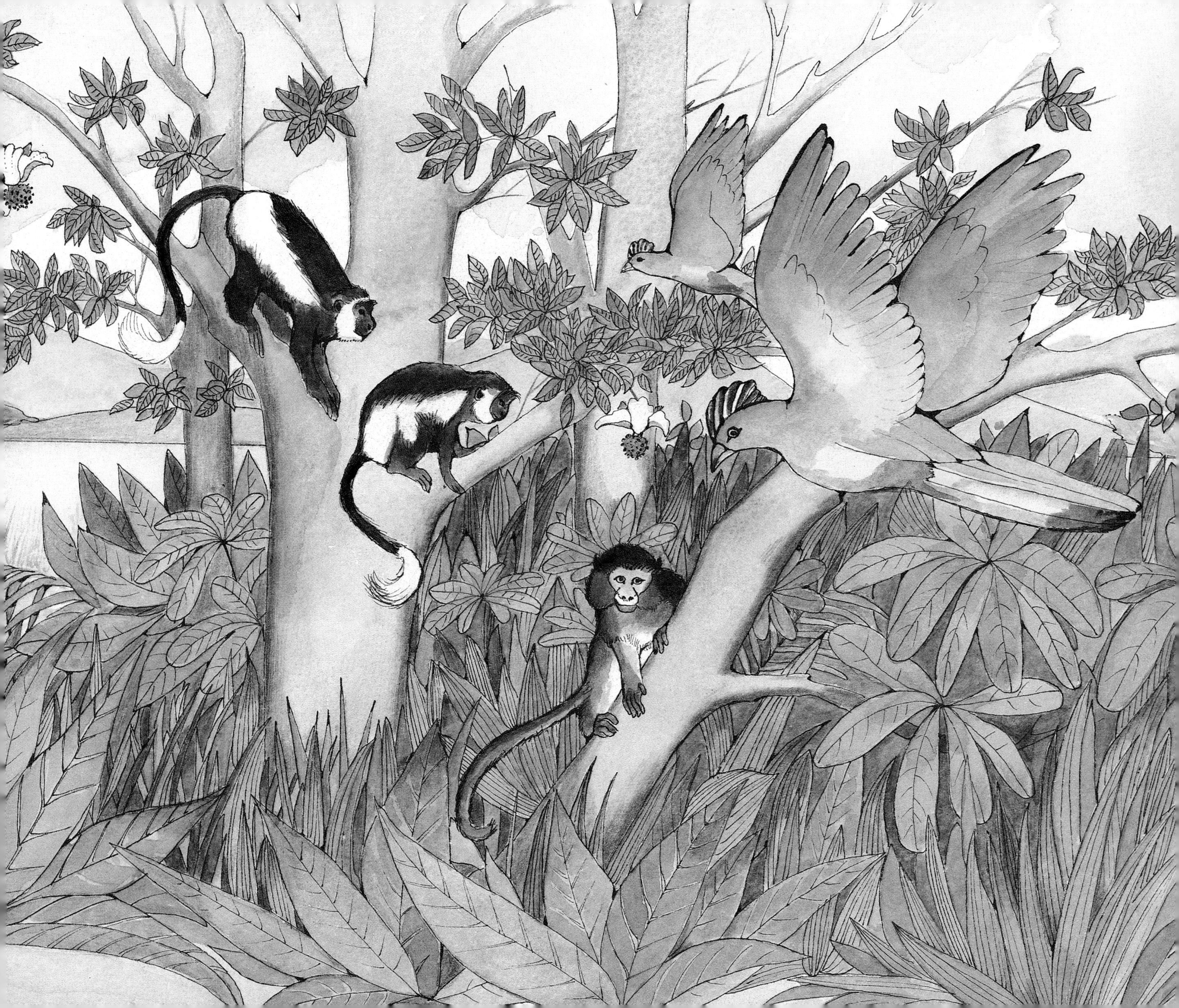

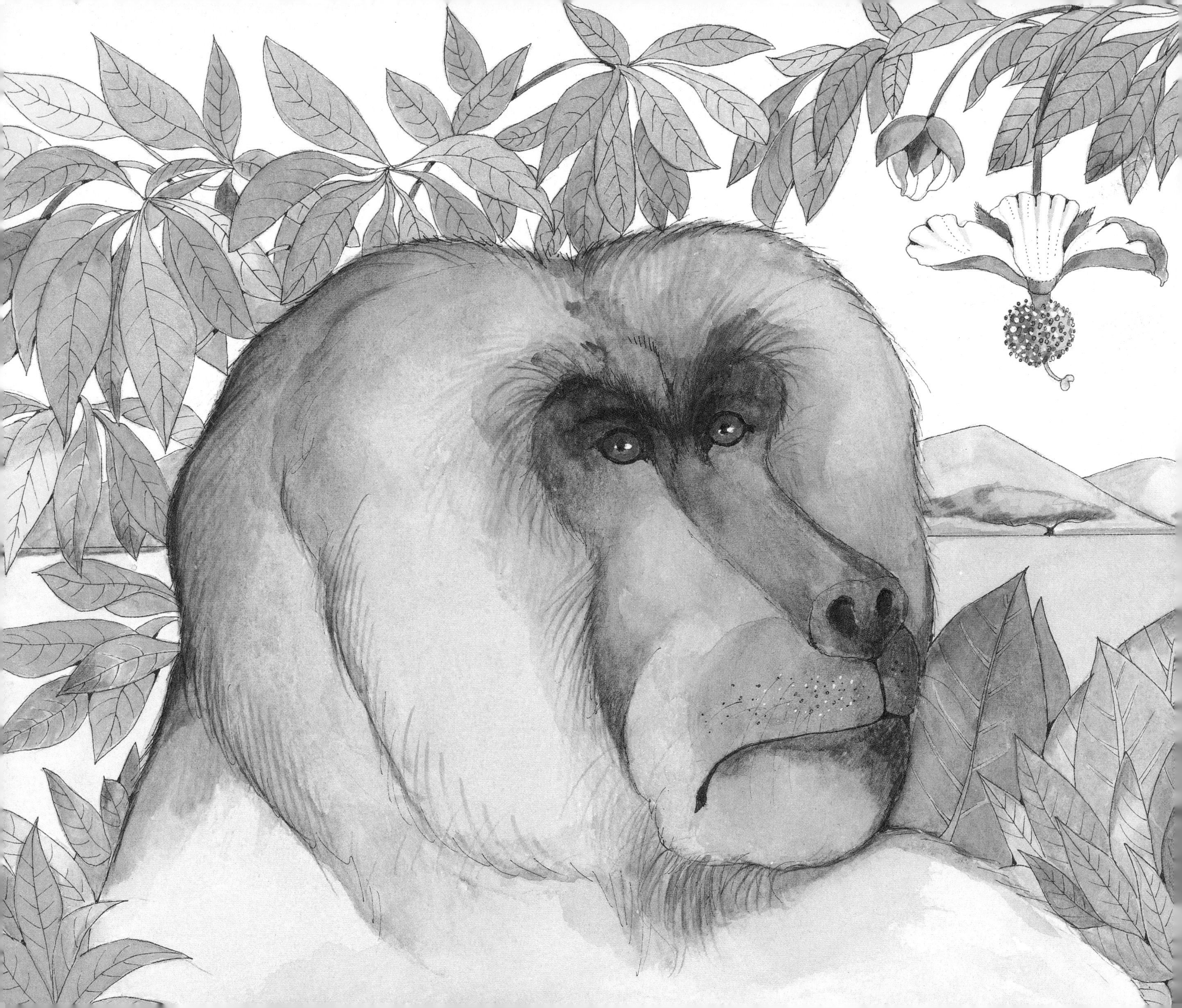

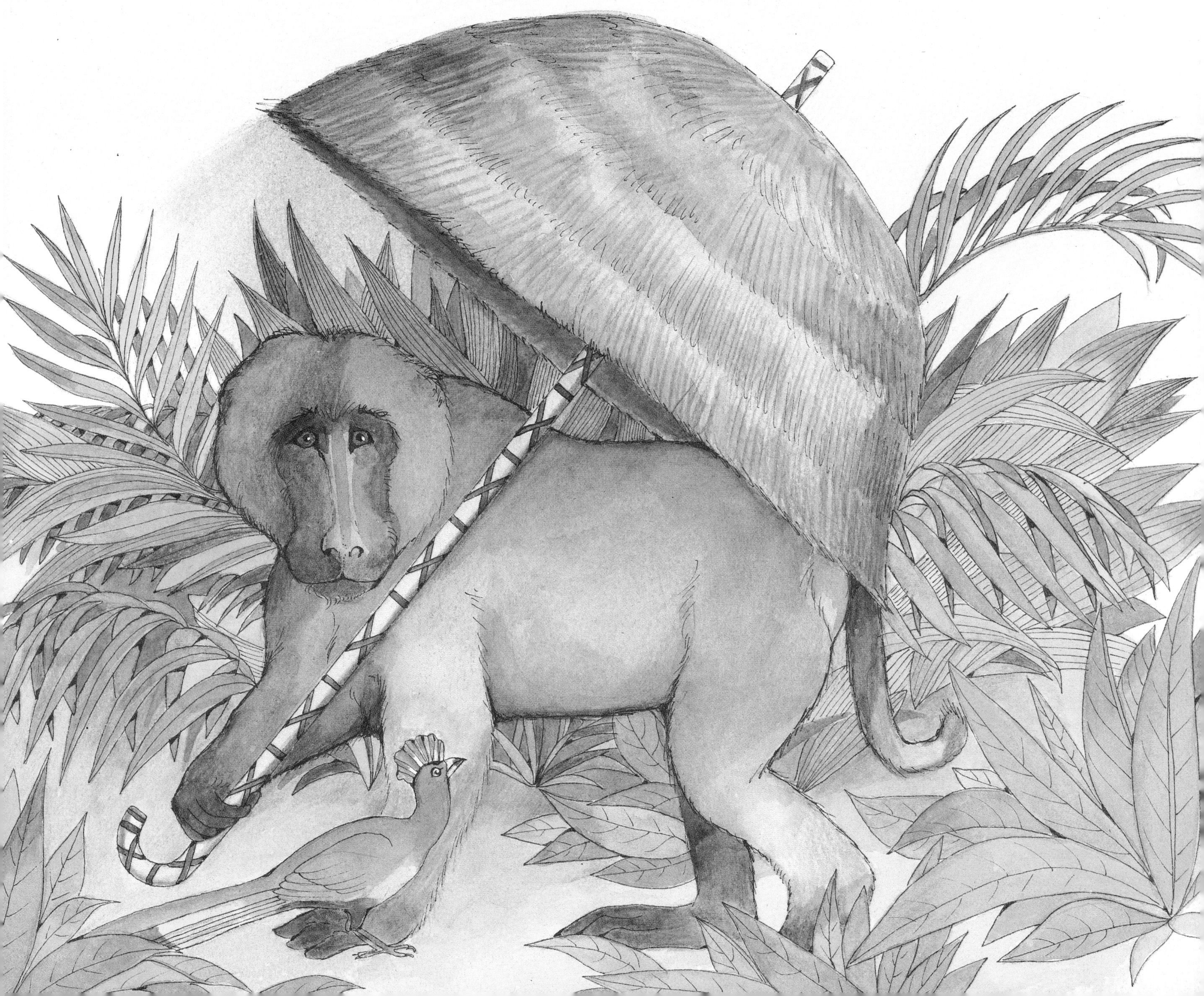

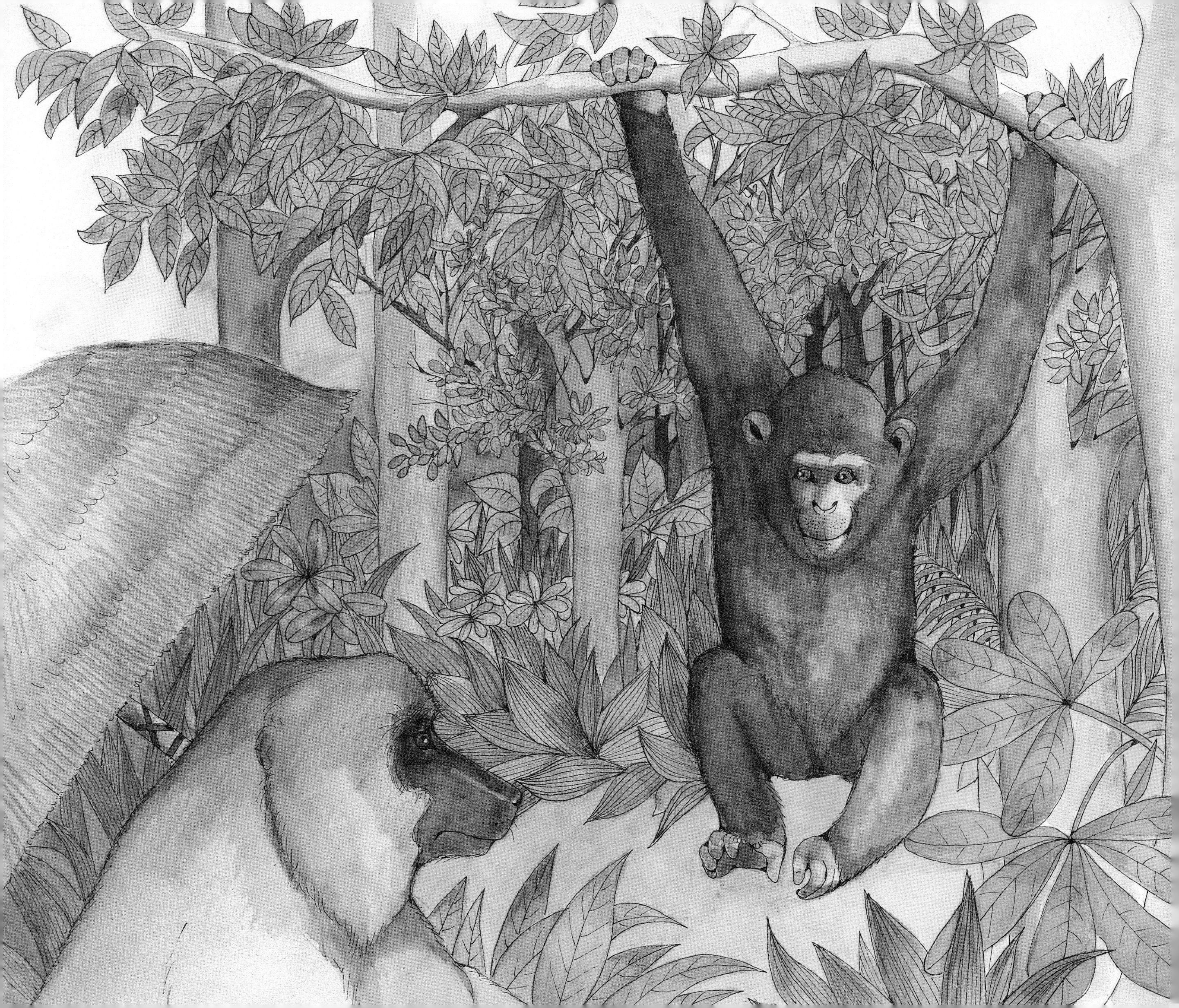

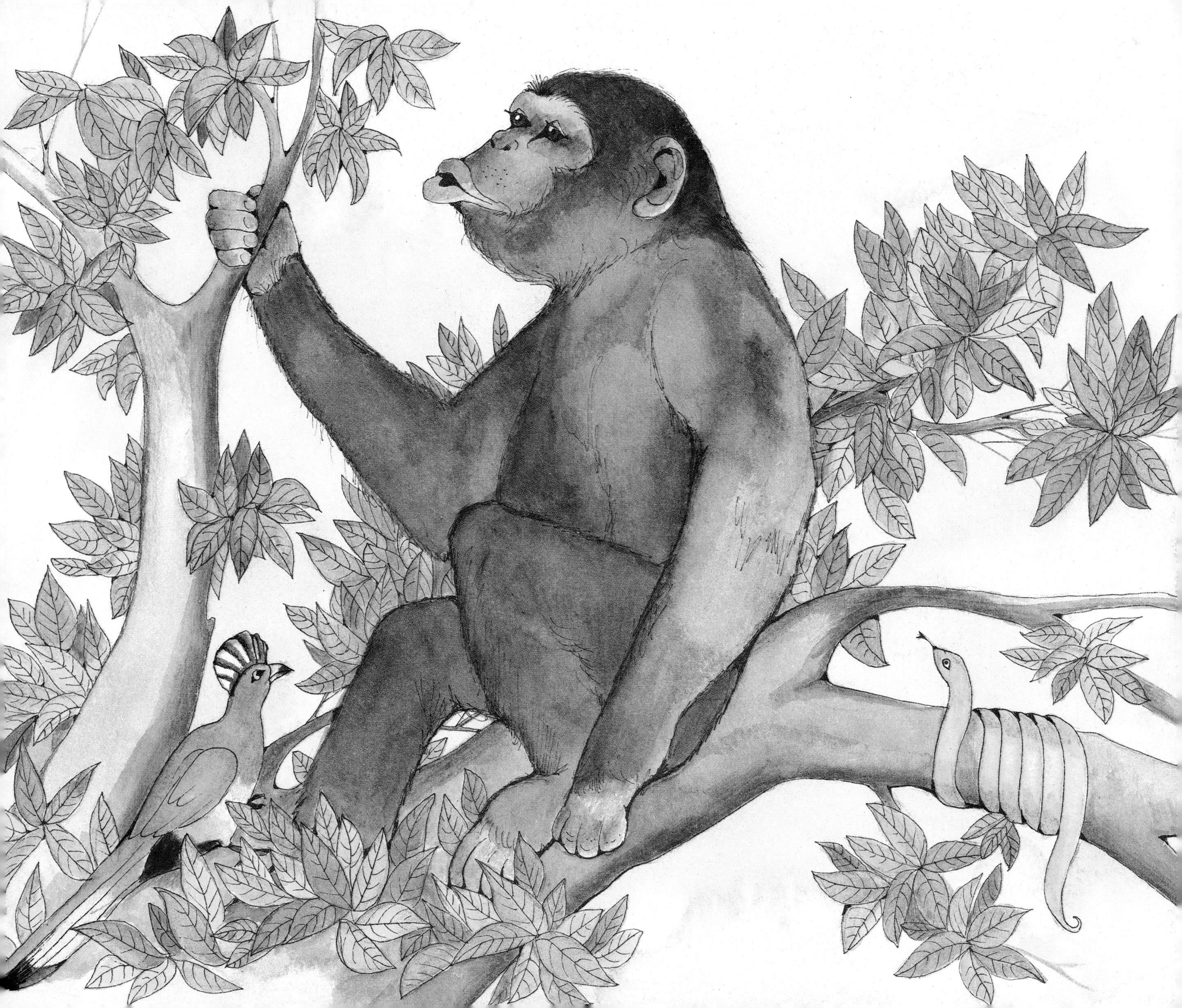

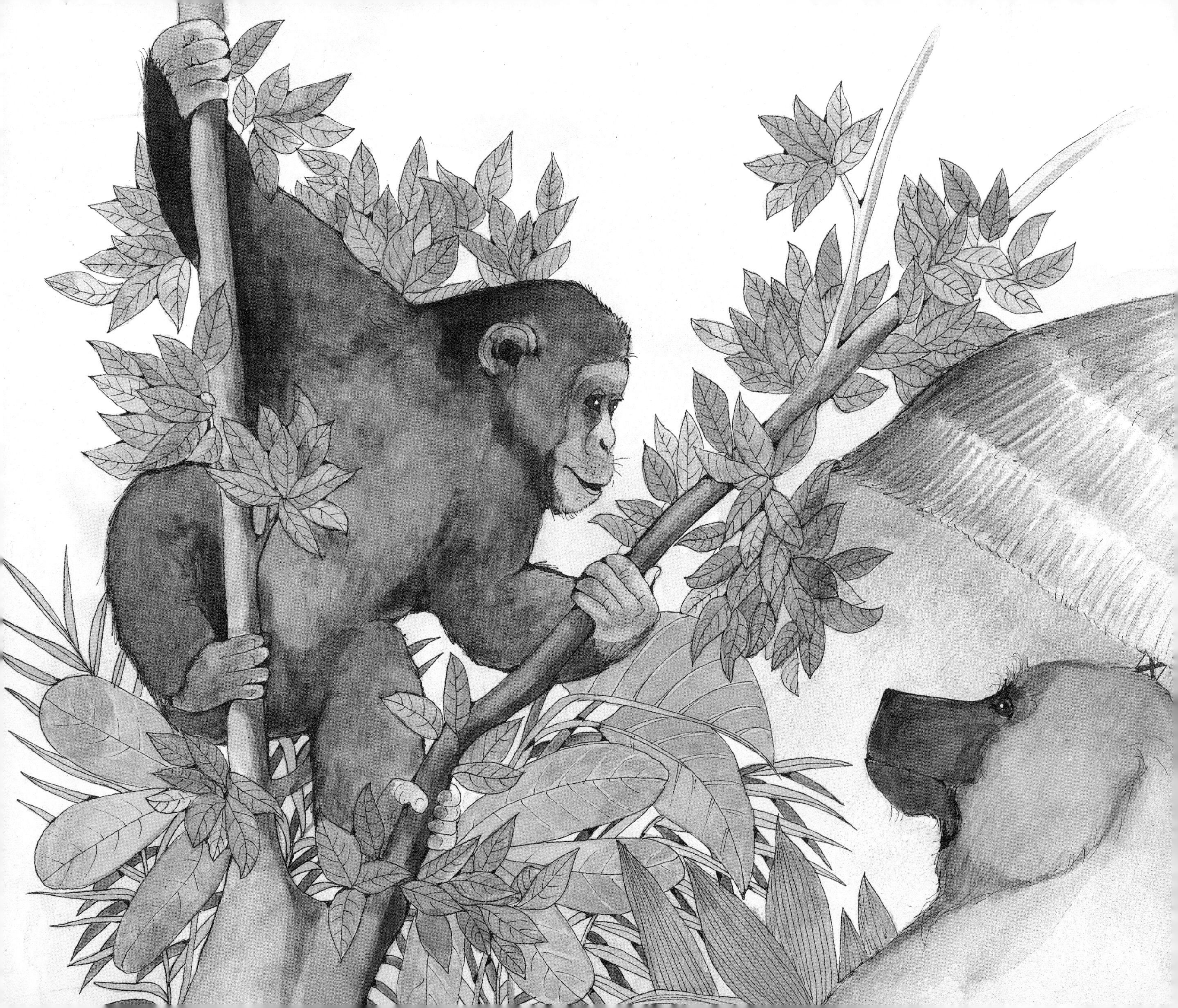

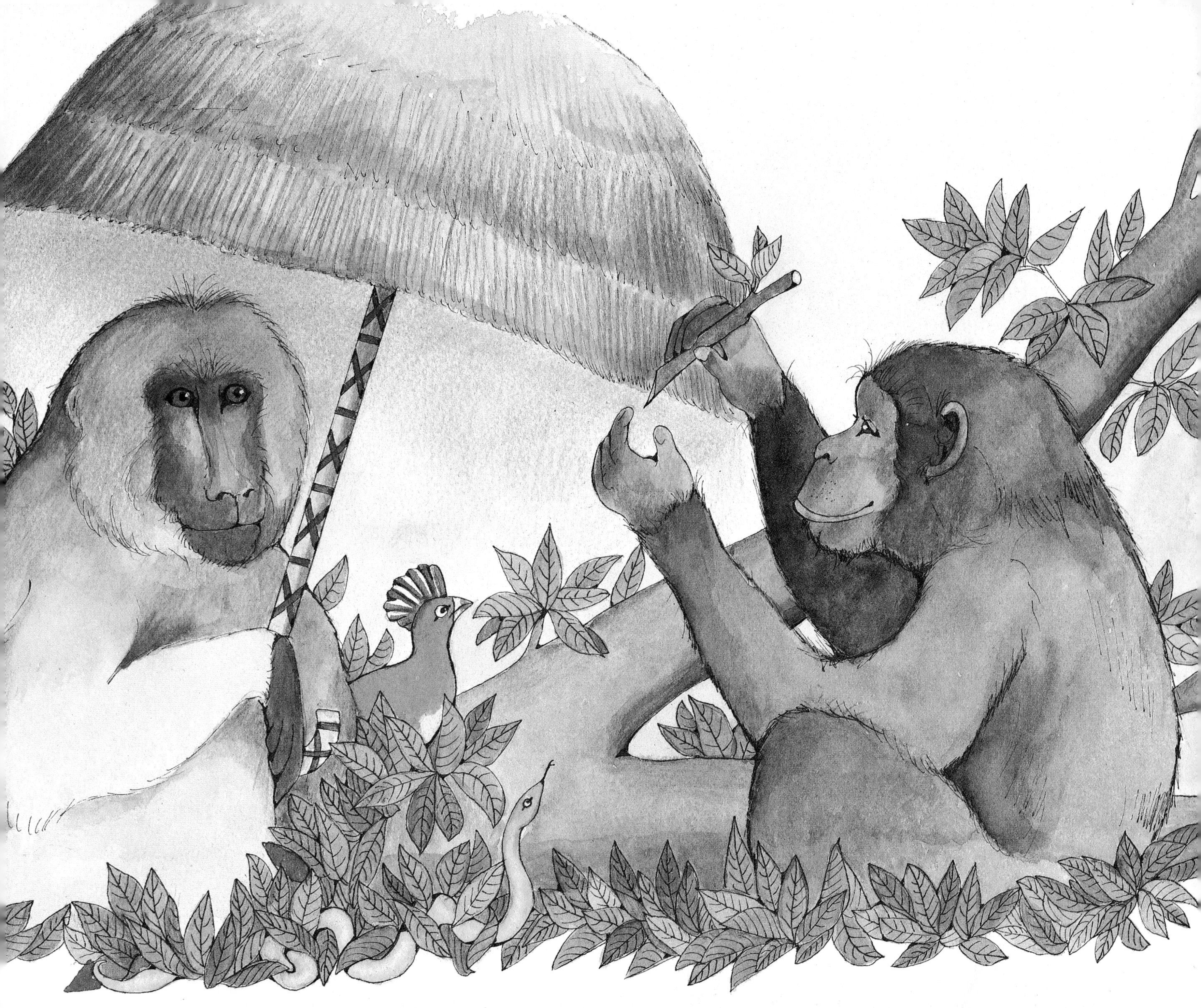

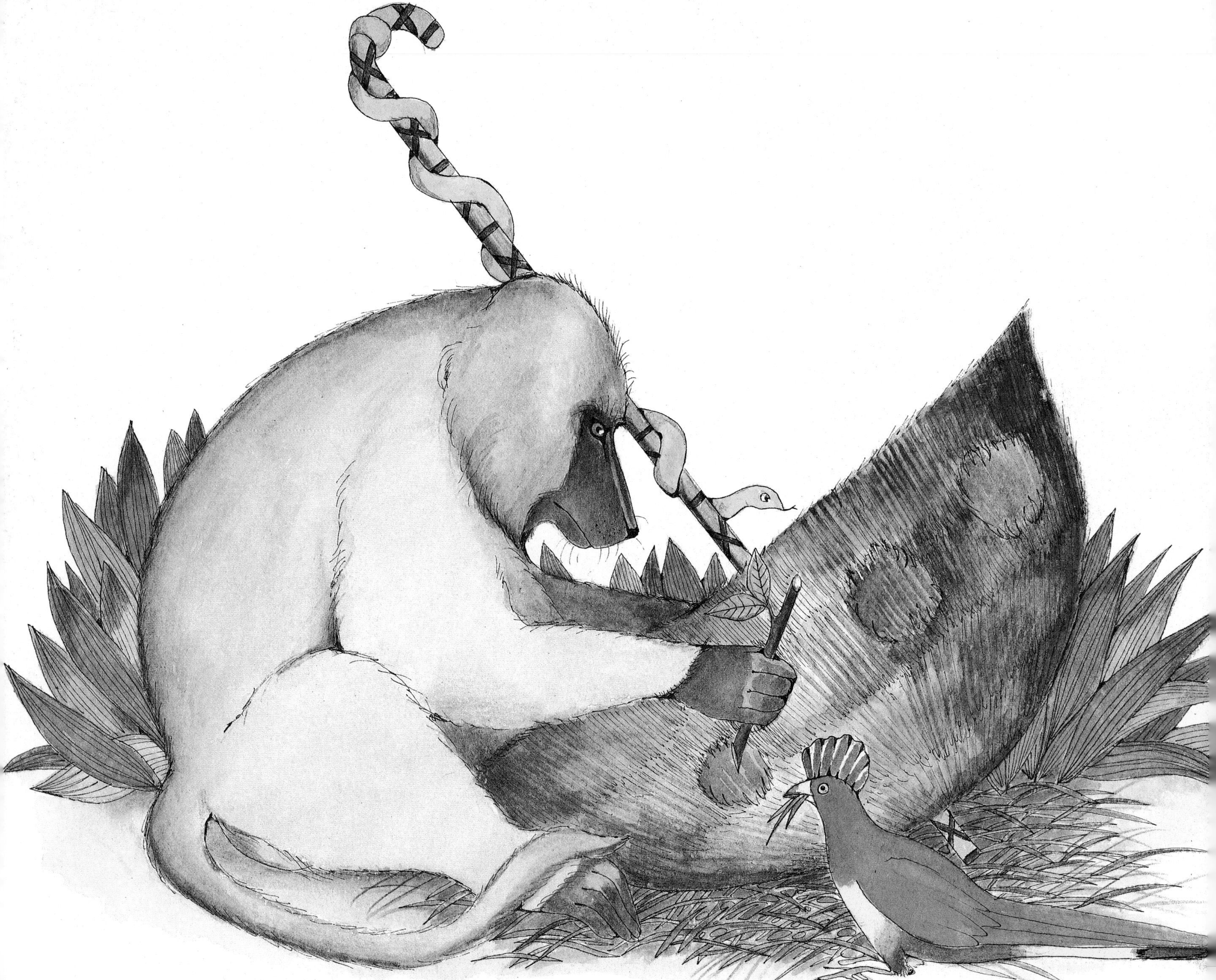

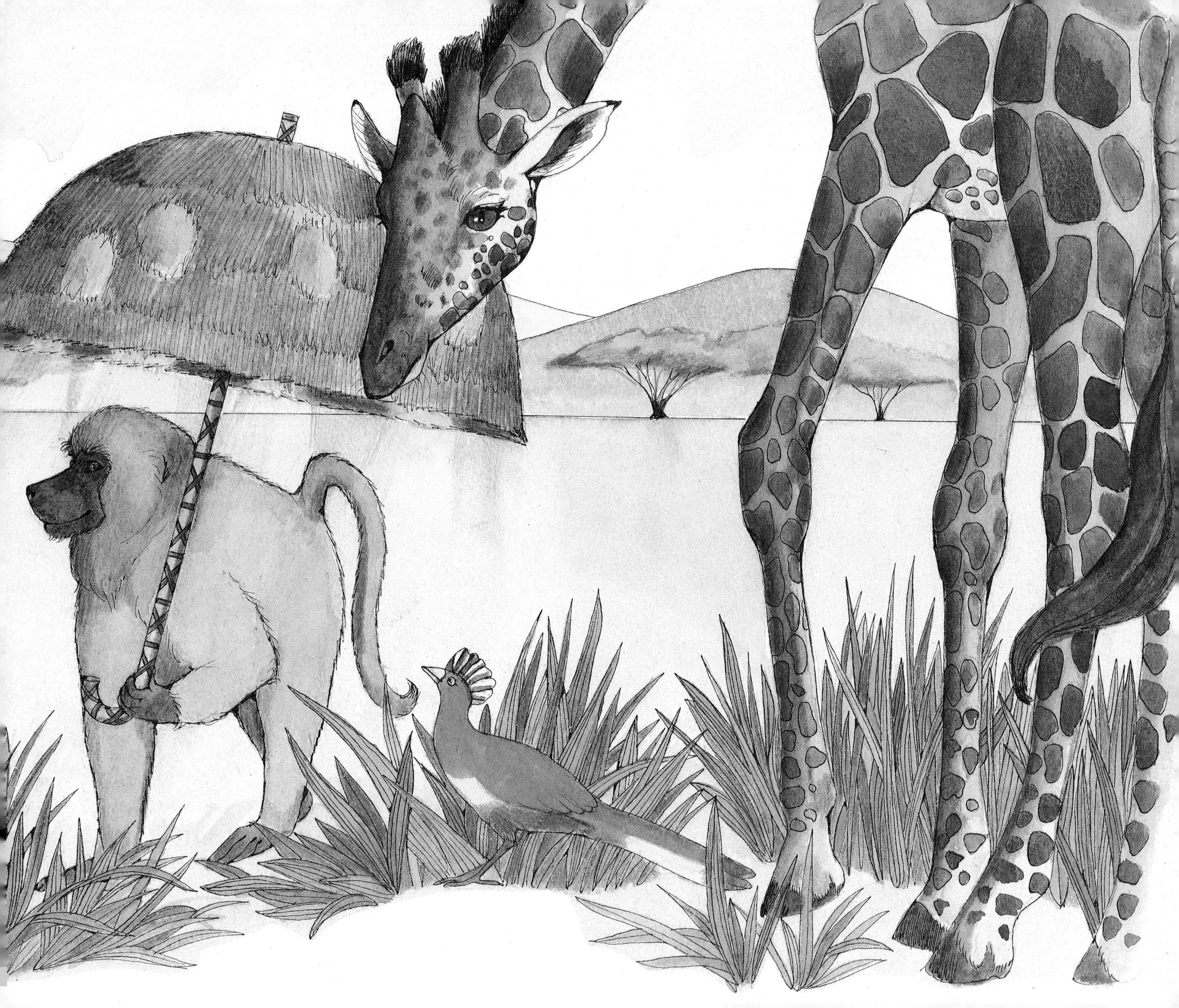

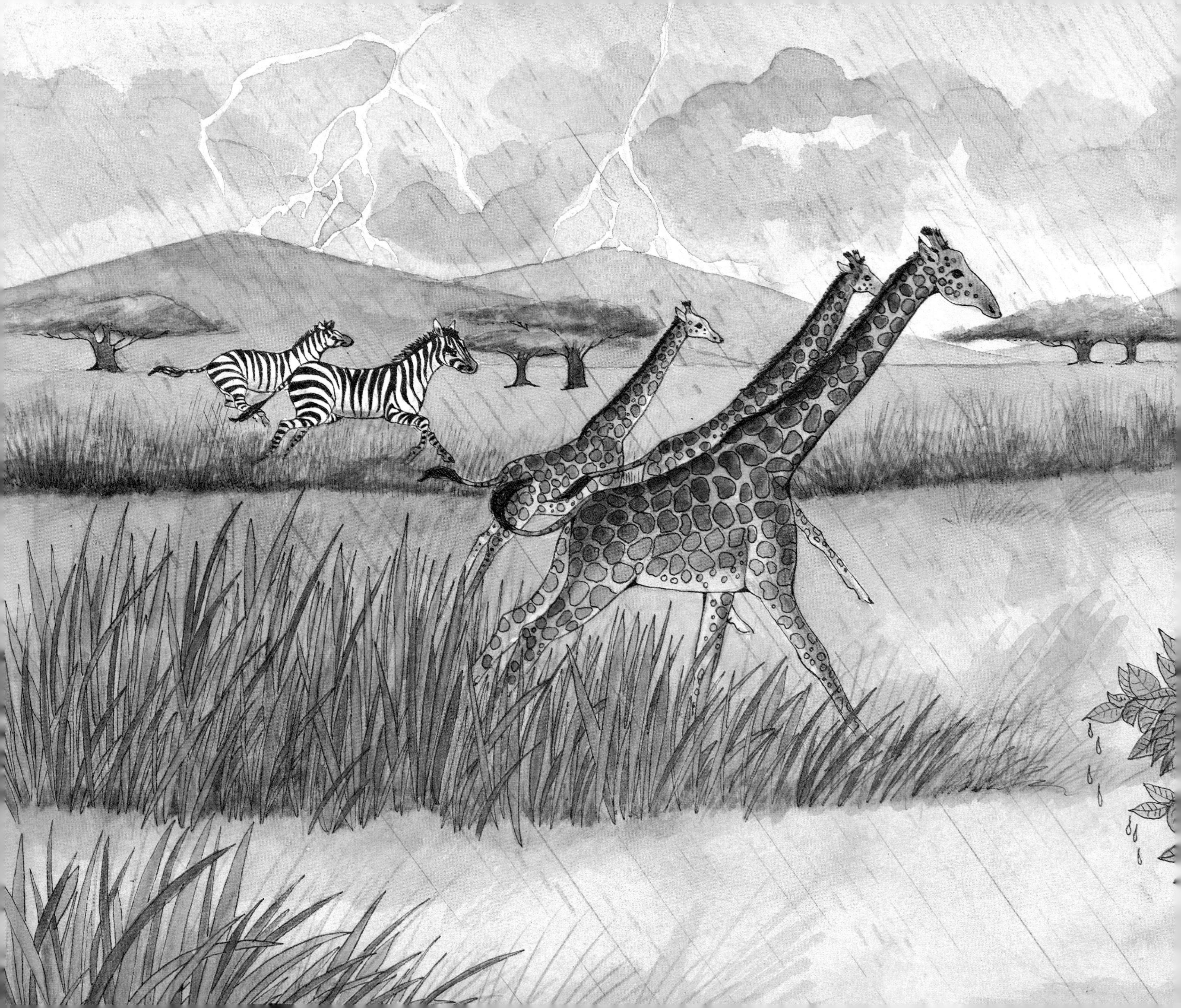

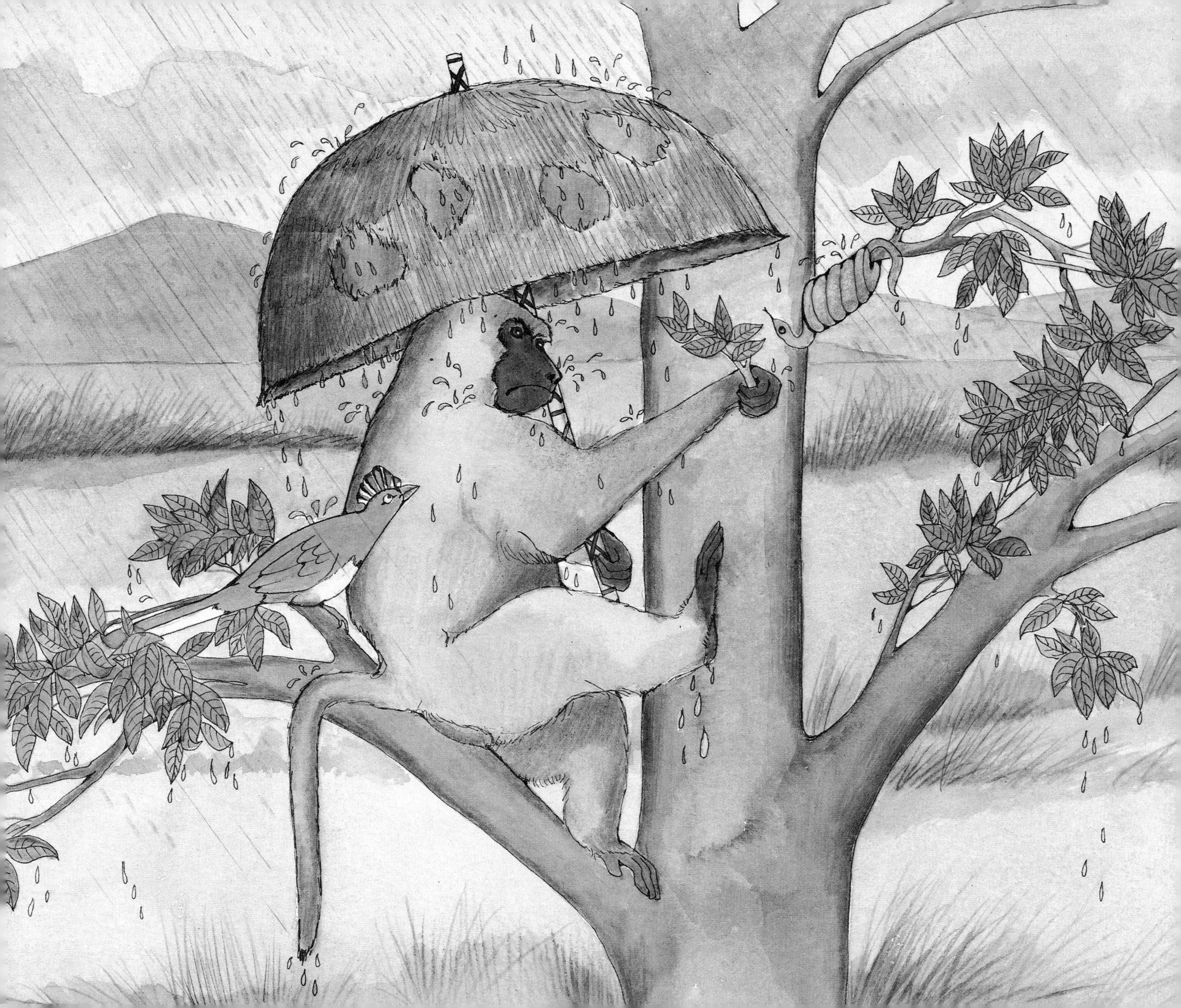

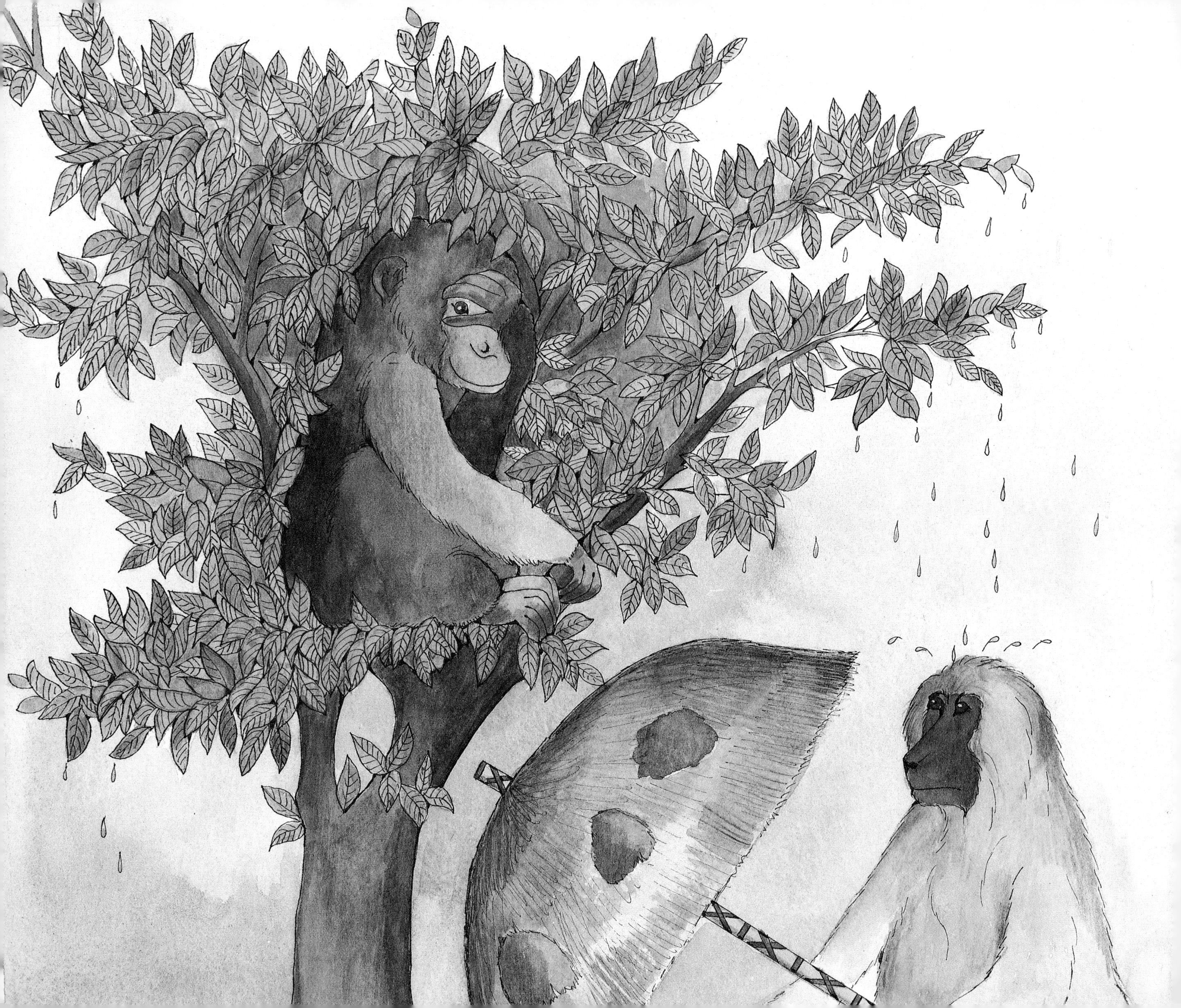

Story text

The baboon is a very responsible animal. Whenever he goes out into the jungle, he always takes his umbrella with him to make sure that, if it rains, he won't get wet.

One morning, baboon got out of bed and found that his umbrella would not close. He tried and tried to get the umbrella to go down but it wouldn't. So, baboon had to go into the jungle with his umbrella up.

The sun was shining, the birds were singing in the treetops, and the other monkeys were swinging around, but the baboon was very unhappy. His umbrella would not go down. He had to stand in the shade. He couldn't feel any of the warm sunlight.

Before too long, baboon ran into a friendly chimpanzee who was swinging in the treetops.

Chimpanzee said to him, "Mr. Baboon, what are you doing with your umbrella open? Why don't you put it down? It's beautiful outside."

The Baboon said, "I would close it if I could, but it's stuck open."

"I have an idea," said chimpanzee. "Why don't you cut holes in the top? Then you'll be able to feel the sun come shining through."

"Why, that's a very good idea," said baboon.

So, baboon cut huge holes in the top of the umbrella and put it over his head. Soon he could feel the warm sun shining on his shaggy head.

But before too long, thunderclouds rolled over the jungle and it began to rain. Even though baboon had his umbrella up, the rain kept dripping through the holes. It ran down his shaggy head and onto his shaggy chin. He got soaking wet.

And so it would seem, the advice of friends is like the weather: sometimes good, sometimes bad.

Project Editor: Alice Flanagan
Design and Electronic Page Composition: Biner Design
Engraver: Liberty Photoengravers

About the storyteller

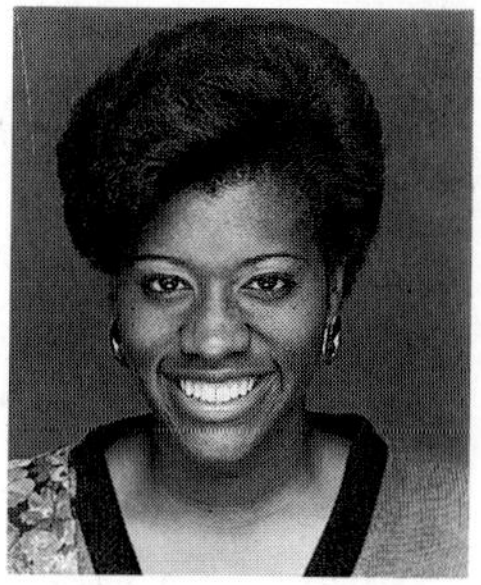

My name is Donna Lanette Washington. I am the storyteller you hear on the tape recording of *The Baboon's Umbrella*.

I have loved stories ever since I was very young. Every night at dinnertime, during dessert, my father would sit at the head of the table and tell stories. That was when I discovered that I could travel around the world and through time without leaving my chair.

When I began college at Northwestern University, the world of storytelling was reopened for me. Once again I could feel the magic of stories. It was at this time that I decided to bring the magic to others.

Since I graduated from college I have shared many stories with many people. I hope you have enjoyed hearing the story I have told you and will want to share it with others.

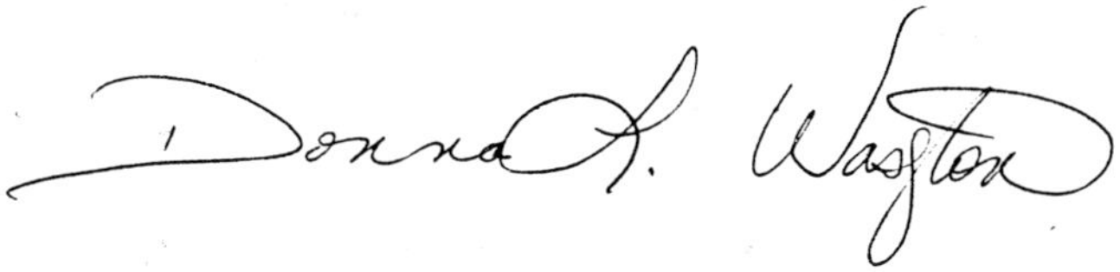

About the illustrator

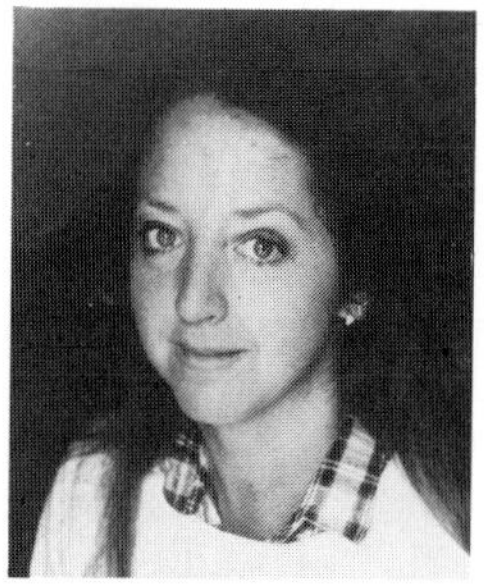

I have been an artist and designer for more than twenty years. Many of the animals and wildlife scenes I have drawn appear on greeting cards, postage stamps, and in children's books.

I enjoyed painting the characters for *The Baboon's Umbrella* because the story is so light-hearted and the animals are charming.

Besides being an artist, I am a licensed glider pilot, a certified scuba diver, and an English horseback riding instructor. I also love to work in my garden at my home in St. Louis, Missouri, which I share with my husband and our dog "Sandy."

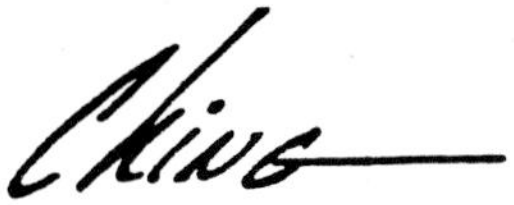

Storytelling activities

Storytelling provides a wonderful opportunity to share information, feelings, and a love of books with children. Through listening, discussion, and a wide variety of post-story activities, children can be helped to understand new ideas, learn and use new words, practice listening skills, experience life outside the dominant culture, and develop writing and storytelling skills. Some of the following activities may be helpful in making this possible:

- Discuss the story. This will give children the opportunity to ask questions and share information they have learned.

- Ask children to retell the story. This will help you measure their comprehension and interact with them through quiet conversation.

- Ask children to act out the story. Provide generic props (scarves, crowns, masks) and puppets.

- Have paper and magic markers or crayons available so children can draw the story. You might ask them to draw a picture of one of the characters in the book or make a story map (a series of drawings reflecting the sequence of story events).

- Ask children to make cutouts of the story characters and back them with felt or flannel for use on a felt/flannel board. As you retell the story, place the cutouts on the board; then ask the children to retell the story several times. Afterwards, comment on their personal variations.

- Help children write a letter to a favorite story character; or have them pretend to be one of the characters in the story and write a letter to you.

- Ask children to tell the story from different points of view. Have them retell the story several times — each time basing it on the viewpoint of a different character.

- Play the "what if" game. Ask children to tell how the story would be different if the hero was a girl instead of a boy; if the ending changed; if the story took place today instead of "once upon a time"; if the story took place in a different country.

More about storytelling and folktales

If you'd like to read more about storytelling or other African folktales, check out some of the following books from your local library:

Breneman, Lucille N. and Bren Breneman. *Once Upon a Time: A Storytelling Handbook.* Chicago: Nelson-Hall, 1983.

Schimmel, Nancy. *Just Enough to Make a Story.* Berkeley, CA: Sisters' Choice Press, 1982.

Sierra, Judy. *Twice Upon a Time: Stories to Tell, Retell, Act Out and Write About.* New York: H. W. Wilson, 1989.

Sierra, Judy. *The Flannel Board Storytelling Book.* New York: H. W. Wilson, 1987.

Arnott, Kathleen. *African Myths and Legends.* New York: Henry Z. Walck, 1962.

Green, Lila. *Tales from Africa,* selected and retold. Silver Burdett, 1979.

Pitcher, Diana. *Tokoloshi: African Folk-Tale*s, adapted and retold. Celestial Arts, 1981.

Library of Congress Cataloging-in-Publication Data
Ching.
    The baboon's umbrella / illustrated by Mary "Ching" Walters.
        p. cm. — (Adventures in storytelling)
    Summary: An African fable about a baboon who, in an effort to protect himself from the rain, follows the sincere but foolish advice of a friendly chimpanzee. Provides a list for adults of storytelling activities.
        ISBN 0-516-05131-8
        [1. Fables. 2. Folklore—Africa.] I. Title. II. Series.
PZ8.2.C48bab   1991
398.2—dc20   91-7952
[E]   CIP
                                                          AC

Copyright © 1991 by Childrens Press ®, Inc.
All rights reserved. Published simultaneously in Canada.
Printed in the United States of America.
1 2 3 4 5 6 7 8 9 10 R 99 98 97 96 95 94 93 92 91 90